Disney's

DOUG™

Created by
Jim Jinkins

CHRONICLES

Winter
Games

by Tim Grundmann

Illustrated by
Kevin Kobasic

Winter Games is hand-illustrated by the same
Grade A Quality Jumbo artist who brings you
Disney's Doug, the television series.

DISNEY
PRESS

New York

Original characters for "The Funnies" developed by Jim Jinkins and
Joe Aaron.

Printed in the United States of America.

The artwork for this book was prepared using watercolor.

The text for this book is set in 18-point New Century Schoolbook.

ISBN: 0-7868-4264-4

Winter Games

CHAPTER 1

"Hey, Doug, watch out!" Skeeter
Valentine shouted. "Roger's
behind that tree and he's got a—"
   POW!
   Right on Doug's back!
   "A snowball, Skeeter?" Doug
asked.
   "Yeah," Skeeter said. "Watch out
for it!"

1

Roger Klotz popped out from behind a tree. "Too bad they don't give medals for snowball-throwing, Funnie." He laughed. "'Cause I'd be takin' home the gold!"

Then Doug's eyes lit up. "Roger, that's it!"

Roger looked confused. "It is? I mean, of course it is. Er, *what's* it?"

"Mayor Tippy asked us to think of ways to raise money for charity, right?" Doug said. "C'mon, guys, we're late already."

They ran two blocks all the way to the Moody School. The meeting was just starting when they got to the auditorium. First, Mayor Tippy Dink thanked all the kids for coming. Then she got down to business.

"I'm sure you've all got great ideas for our winter charity drive," she said. "So let's get started."

Just then the Sleech brothers came out on the stage. They were wheeling a huge machine with blinking lights.

"Excuse the interruption," Al Sleech said. "But perhaps our new invention can be of help."

"Behold the Ideometer!" Moo Sleech shouted.

Al explained that the wires were attached to the brains of two great geniuses. "They will judge the best idea," he said.

"Er, may I ask where you got the brains?" Mayor Tippy asked.

"No!" the Sleech brothers said quickly, looking at one another in a panic. But then Mayor Tippy noticed the wires attached to their own heads.

"Okay," she said smiling, "who'd like to go first? Connie?"

Connie Benge said they could collect empty soda bottles. The Ideometer whirred and sputtered.

"Bo-ring!"
it said.

Chalky
Studebaker
said they
could have
a car wash.
The Ideometer
said, *"It's too cold to wash cars in the winter!"*

Then Doug told his idea.
"We could have a whole day of winter sports. Snowball-throwing, snowman-making, and skeeting."

"Skeeting?" Mayor Tippy asked.
"Don't you mean skating?"

"No, skeeting," Patti

6

Mayonnaise said. "It's like skating, only you wear shoes."

Al Sleech nodded. "Skeeter, the Great One, invented it one day when he forgot to bring his skates."

"His brain power is even mightier than ours!" Moo Sleech added.

The Ideometer whirred and

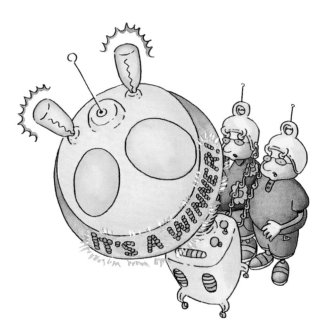

sputtered as it considered Doug's idea. *"It's a winner!"* it said.

"Congratulations, Doug," Mayor Tippy said. "The Bluffington Winter Games it is!"

Doug couldn't believe it. His idea was a winner! And all because of Roger and his snow-ball.

CHAPTER 2

At Swirly's the next day, Patti popped the question.

"Hey, Doug," she said, "are you planning on entering the skeeting contest?"

"Sure am," he said. "Why, Patti?"

"I was thinking that we could skeet together," she said. "We could do a pairs routine. How about it?"

Doug couldn't believe it. Patti could have asked Chalky or Guy or lots of other guys. But she asked *him*! He decided to play it cool.

"Uh, sure, Patti," he said. "You want to meet tomorrow at Ducky Luck Flake? I mean, Fluffy Kluck Drake? Er, Lucky Duck Lake? We could start practicing then."

Patti grinned. "Great, Doug. See ya!"

During dinner that night, Doug had the greatest daydream ever. He and Patti were skeeting in the Winter Games, and everyone was

cheering! For their finish, they
jumped in the air, spinning eight
times in slow motion before land-
ing perfectly—with their hands

and feet touching to form a heart. The crowd went wild!

Doug's sister Judy interrupted his daydream. "Well, Dougie," she said, "looks like we'll both be competing in the skeeting contest."

Doug groaned. "Judy, you won't do anything to embarrass me, will you?"

"Who, me?" Judy asked with a playful smile. "How could *I*, Judith the Ice Queen, embarrass *you*?"

"Sorry I asked." Doug sighed.

The next morning, Doug and Porkchop went to Lucky Duck Lake. Patti was already there, practicing her spins. Patti was a great skeeter.

"Hey, Doug, hey, Porkchop!" she called. "You ready, Doug?"

They started out with a few simple moves. Patti did a spin, while Doug jumped up and clicked his heels. But the best part was that Doug got to hold her hands while they skeeted.

"Doug, that's a great move!" Patti said.

Doug blushed. "I call it the Funnie," he said. "I can even do a double-Funnie."

Patti looked unsure. "I don't know, Doug. You might hurt your- self."

"Nah," he said. "Look, I'll show you!"

They started their routine again. Patti broke away to do her spin. Porkchop closed his eyes as Doug jumped as high he could. He clicked his heels once, twice—

Then *crash*, he landed on the ice!

Patti and Porkchop skeeted to

Doug's side. "Doug! Are you all right?" Patti cried.

Doug couldn't answer. His leg hurt so bad, he wanted to holler. But not in front of Patti!

CHAPTER 3

Skeeter looked at Doug's cast and whistled. "Boy, Doug," he said, "you sure are lucky."

Doug groaned. "Lucky? Skeeter, I've got a broken leg!"

"Yeah," said Skeeter, "but now you can draw stuff right on your cast!"

Doug didn't think he was lucky

at all. Now he wouldn't be able to skeet with Patti! He was never so miserable in his life.

Patti came over later that day. She brought Doug a book of puzzles to cheer him up. "That's a great cast, Doug!" she said. "Can I autograph it?"

"I saved you a space, Patti," Doug said. "I guess I shouldn't have tried to do a double-Funnie, huh?"

But Patti only smiled as she signed his cast. Doug was glad she hadn't said, "I told you so." Then he read what she wrote and he laughed. There it was, in big letters: I told you so!

"I guess you heard I'm skeeting with Chalky," Patti said.

"That's great," Doug said. "There's no point in you missing out on the fun." But he couldn't help feeling jealous. "I just wish *I* could enter the games," he sighed.

Patti laughed. "Maybe you can't skeet, Doug, but you can enter the other events. If my dad can, then so can you."

Doug thought a bit. Patti's

father had been in a wheelchair since his car accident years ago. But he still managed to drive a car and even play basketball.

"I guess I can try," Doug said.

Patti went to call her father. When she came back, she was beaming. "My dad's coming over tomorrow with an extra wheelchair, Doug. He'll show you how to get around."

Doug wasn't so sure. But Patti had already made the arrangements. He didn't want to disappoint her.

"Come on, Doug," Mr. Mayonnaise said, "don't give up."

Doug groaned, "My arms are getting sore."

Mr. Mayonnaise chuckled. "I know what you mean. You're using muscles you didn't know you had. Try it again."

Doug spent a half hour practicing in the wheelchair. He was

surprised how hard it was. The wheels felt so heavy because he had to push his own weight.

"It took *me* a while to get used to it, too," Mr. Mayonnaise said. "That's enough for today, Doug. Keep working on it, okay?"

Doug smiled. "Thanks a lot, Mr. Mayonnaise."

Doug went into the house to get a drink of water. "Need some help, Douglas?" his mother asked.

"No, thanks, Mom," he said. "I've got to learn to do things for myself."

Mrs. Funnie smiled and left the kitchen. Porkchop watched nervously as Doug reached inside the

cabinet. The glass tipped over and—

SMASH!

Doug sighed at the broken pieces of glass on the floor. "I can't even get a glass of water," he said. "How can I build a snowman or throw a snowball?"

The next day, Doug's arms ached even more. He went outside to practice for the contest. Porkchop stood nervously with an apple on his head as Doug took aim with a snowball.

"Ready, aim . . . " he said, then pitched.

WHOOSH!

"Missed by a mile," Doug groaned. "It's a lot harder to throw sitting down."

But Porkchop breathed a sigh of relief.

Then Doug tried making a snowman in the shape of Porkchop. But it took too long and

his back got sore from bending over to pick up the snow.

"It's hopeless, Porkchop," Doug said. "Why did this have to happen two days before the Winter Games? It isn't fair!"

CHAPTER 4

Everyone cheered as Mayor Tippy
Dink ran to the entrance of the
park. She carried the Eternal
Snow Cone, the symbol of the
Bluffington Winter Games.

She gasped for breath and said,
"Let . . . (puff-puff) . . . the games
. . . (puff-puff) . . . begin!"

The crowd broke into applause.
"Yaaay!"

"The things I do for this town," Mayor Tippy murmured.

Everyone went off to watch the snowball-throwing contest. Everyone except Doug. Patti's dad came up and said, "Come on, Doug! Aren't you entering?"

Doug shook his head. "I can't throw very well sitting down," he said.

"Have you tried it?" Mr. Mayonnaise asked.

Doug nodded. "Now my arms are sore," he complained.

"Well, you have a few minutes if you decide to change your mind," Mr. Mayonnaise said as he wheeled off. Doug pushed his wheelchair to the Snow-Snacks stand. He bought two chocolate-covered icicles. He handed one to Porkchop and said, "Some fun, huh, pal?"

But Porkchop was having fun. He built a snow fort while

Doug moped in his wheelchair.

Later, Doug watched the snow-people-making contest. Skeeter was making a snow statue of the Lucky Duck Monster. "Aren't you entering, Doug?" he asked.

Doug sighed. "I'm in a wheelchair, Skeet. Remember?"

"You could try," Skeeter said. "You could bend down and grab some snow and—"

But Doug shook his head. "It wouldn't be as good," he said. "And it would take me forever."

Skeeter just shrugged. An hour later, the judging began. Roger's snowman was gigantic. It looked exactly like Roger and it was

looking down at all the other
little people.

"I call it the Colossus of
Bluffington!" he said proudly.

"You made this yourself?" one of
the judges asked.

"Of course I made it," Roger

snapped back. "Who do you think made it—professional snowman makers?"

Three men came up to Roger. They wore caps that read ACE SNOWMAN MAKERS. "Here's our bill, Mr. Klotz," one of them said.

Roger got red in the face. "I don't know what you're talkin' about," he sputtered. But the judges walked away.

Roger got so mad, he kicked the giant snow-Roger in the shin. A big chunk broke off and flattened Skeeter's Lucky Duck Snow Monster.

Roger howled with laughter.

"Valentine, if you could see the look on your—"

SPLAT!

The head of the giant snow-Roger fell on Roger!

"Help!" he shouted. "Get me off of me!"

Skeeter sighed as he looked at his ruined snowman. "Oh, well, I can do it over."

31

Doug didn't know why Skeeter bothered. The judging was over, so what was the point?

"The judges have made their decision. The winner of the snow-people contest is . . . Chalky Studebaker!"

Everyone applauded. Doug

thought Chalky's Giant Quarterback snowman was great. But he thought he could have done better. Maybe a snow-Quailman . . . "If only I didn't have this broken leg," he sighed to Porkchop.

"And now, folks, the figure-skeeting competition is about to begin at Lucky Duck Lake!"

Everyone rushed off. That's when Doug saw Patti's dad making a snowman. It was only half finished, and he was working hard to make it. Doug wasn't sure why, but he felt guilty.

CHAPTER 5

"Ladies and gentlemen . . . please welcome the first figure-skeeting contestant . . . Skeeter Valentine!"

Everyone clapped as Skeeter zipped across the ice.

"He's going to do a figure seven," Connie said. "No one's ever done one before."

Roger laughed. "Yeah, 'cause

no one's goofy enough to try!"

Skeeter skeeted a straight line, making the top of a seven. Then he made a sharp turn to make the bottom part—and he slipped.

"Ohhhhhh," everybody groaned.

But Skeeter didn't seem upset. When he finished, he skeeted to the judges' stand and asked, "Can we count it as a three and a half? That's half a seven."

"And now, performing an original ice-ballet . . . Judy Funnie!"

Doug gulped. He wasn't sure he wanted to watch this.

Three musicians stood at the edge of the ice. One played bongo drums. Another shook a

tambourine. The third crashed
cymbals.

Then Judy skeeted onto the ice
in high heels. She was dressed in
black and carried a basket of ice
cubes.

"Behold the Ice Woman!" the
musicians chanted. "Woe! Woe!
Woe!"

Judy put her hand to her forehead, like she had a headache. Then she stomped on the ice. Doug thought the ice would crack and she'd fall right through.

"Ice of the ages!" Judy screamed. "Ice of doom!" She threw ice cubes at the musicians. "Cold cubes of melty indifference. Ice, begone!!"

Some people started giggling. They thought it was a comedy act. Doug groaned.

Finally Judy took a wilted flower from her basket. She held it to her face, then fell sobbing to the ice. The music stopped.

Judy got up and took a bow.

Most people clapped to be polite. Roger said, "Next time I need a good laugh, I'm giving her a call."

Doug watched from his wheel-chair as dozens of other skeeters took to the ice. Then Mayor Tippy announced the final contestants: *"Patti Mayonnaise and Chalky Studebaker!"*

Patti and Chalky skeeted to a

romantic waltz. Doug couldn't help feeling jealous. If he hadn't tried to show off, it would have been *him* out there with Patti.

They finished to a roar of applause. Then the judges cast their votes. *"The winners of the*

skeeting contest . . . Patti Mayonnaise and Chalky Studebaker!"

Everyone applauded as Patti and Chalky accepted their trophy. As they left the ice, Doug congratulated them. "You guys were great!"

"Thanks, Doug!" Chalky said as he rushed off. "Excuse me, but I'm  late for the bobwhitesled warm-up. See ya!"

But Patti stayed. "That's nice of you to say that,

Doug," she said. "That was going to be our routine. But we'll do it next year, okay?"

"You've got a deal," Doug smiled. Good old Patti, he thought. She always had a way of making him feel better.

"You entering the bobwhitesled contest?" she asked.

Doug shook his head. "I probably couldn't fit in the sled with my cast," he said.

Patti looked as if she were about to say something. But she just gave Doug a pat on his shoulder and ran off.

CHAPTER 6

Then came the main event: the bobwhitesled competition.

The bobwhitesleds were just like bobsleds but they had the face of Principal Bob White on the front.

Roger and Stinky were the first team. "Check this out, Funnie," Roger called. "Cell phone, TV,

VCR, computer with CD-ROM, reclining seats with Magic Massage Fingers—the works!"

Stinky was sitting behind Roger. She looked at Porkchop and gave him a "Pfft!" Porkchop growled.

Then Principal White raised the starting flag. "Before we begin, I'd just like to remind everyone that elections are coming up, so don't forget—"

"Get on with it!" everyone shouted.

"On your mark, get set, vote for me! I mean, *go!*"

Roger pushed his bobwhitesled. But it was so overloaded with gadgets that it wouldn't budge. He panicked. "C'mon, Stinky! We've got to get rid of this junk!"

They tossed out the cell phone, the computer, the TV, and VCR. Stinky tossed out her *Cat Today* magazine, her scratching post, and her litter box.

Then Roger tossed out Stinky. "Sorry, pal!" he shouted.

Roger gave his

bobwhitesled a running push, then hopped inside.

"*Joeycookamonga!*" he shouted. And he was off!

Roger zipped down the first hill of the course and disappeared from sight. "No way he'll win," Skeeter said. "He lost a lot of time at the start."

Patti's dad wheeled up beside Doug. "Hey, Doug," he said, "I'm going next. Want to team up?"

Doug shook his head. "No, thanks, I'll just watch."

Mr. Mayonnaise nodded and wheeled over to the starting line. "Need some help, Mr. Mayonnaise?" Skeeter asked.

"Sure, Skeeter," he said. "How about a push?"

Doug watched as Patti's dad lifted himself from his wheelchair into the bobwhitesled. He remembered how hard Mr. Mayonnaise had worked to make a snowman.

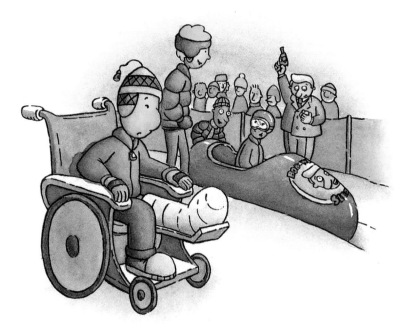

Skeeter had worked hard, too. He didn't stop when his snowman was ruined—he just started over again. And he wasn't miserable that he didn't do his figure seven. He was happy he had done *half* a seven.

Even Roger hadn't quit the bobwhitesled race when he was way behind. And Judy didn't quit skeeting when people laughed. At least they all had tried and *they* were having fun.

Doug hadn't even tried and he realized that's why he was miserable. He had been feeling sorry for himself.

Doug wheeled over to Patti's

dad and asked, "Still got room for me, Mr. Mayonnaise?"

Chad Mayonnaise smiled. "You bet! Hop in, Doug."

Doug climbed out of the wheelchair and slid awkwardly into the back of the bobwhitesled. "Way to go, Doug!" Patti called.

Doug grinned as he put on his

helmet. "Wish us luck, Porkchop!" he called. Porkchop gave Doug a thumbs-up.

Patti, Skeeter, and Chalky all got into position to push the bob-whitesled. Principal White raised his starting flag.

"On your mark . . . get set . . . vote for me! I mean, *go!*"

CHAPTER 7

They were off!

Doug gasped. He was shocked by how fast the bobwhitesled flew down the snowy course. He had to remember to move with the curves or they'd topple over.

"How're you doing back there?" Mr. Mayonnaise shouted.

"Great!" Doug shouted back.

It was kind of scary when they

took those curves, but Doug moved perfectly. It was more fun than any ride at Funkytown!

As they zipped along the course, Doug forgot all about his broken leg. He forgot about his sore arms and the wheelchair. He forgot everything except for the great time he was having.

Patti's dad steered expertly through the course. "Another curve coming up, Doug! Lean in!"

Doug braced himself. They went up . . . and up . . . then zoomed sideways on the wall of the course. Doug loved the spray of snow against his face. There was nothing like it!

Finally the bobwhitesled came to the finish line. Doug's parents rushed over to congratulate him. "I'm so proud of you, Douglas!" his mom said, and gave him a hug.

"Aw, Mom!" Doug said. "All my friends are looking!"

Patti hugged Doug next. (Doug didn't mind that at all!)

Two more teams competed in the race. And then it was time to announce the winners.

"And the first prize winners are Skeeter and Dale Valentine!"

Everyone applauded. Doug was happy for Skeeter and his brother, Dale. They had practiced all week. They deserved it.

"Second place winners . . . Doug Funnie and Chad Mayonnaise!"

Doug couldn't believe it. He hadn't won a sports prize since . . . well, practically forever. And now he had won with a broken leg!

After they got their trophy,

Patti's dad asked Doug if he wanted to keep it at his house.

"Yeah, sure, Mr. Mayonnaise," Doug said. "That way, whenever I look at it, I'll remember not to give up so easily."

"*And* how much fun we had," Mr. Mayonnaise added.

"You bet!" Doug smiled, and they slapped their hands in the air.

Doug thought the second-prize trophy was better than the first-prize one. It was smaller, but filled to the brim with Peanutty Buddies. Porkchop was already licking his lips!

Dear Journal:
It's funny how things turn out. Sure, it's harder to do stuff in a wheelchair, but that's probably because I needed more practice. Skeeter's coming over. We're going outside and I'm finally gonna make that snowman!

I think Porkchop learned something, too: don't eat a dozen Peanutty Buddy cones in one sitting. Poor guy. I hate to see him with a stomachache!

WHOOPS!

Doug was about to take the attendance list to the school office. But he tripped in a trash can. Now all of the names are mixed up. He can't turn them over to Vice Principal Bone like that! Can you help Doug unscramble the names of all the kids in his class?

1. UDGO
2. TIATP
3. EGORR
4. KETRESE
5. YLAKHC
6. OMOBER
7. EDN
8. LYILW
9. NIENCO
10. NKUKSY
11. CKTUNREF
12. EBEEB

1. Doug 2. Patti 3. Roger 4. Skeeter 5. Chalky 6. Boomer 7. Ned 8. Willy 9. Connie 10. Skunky 11. Fentruck 12. Beebe

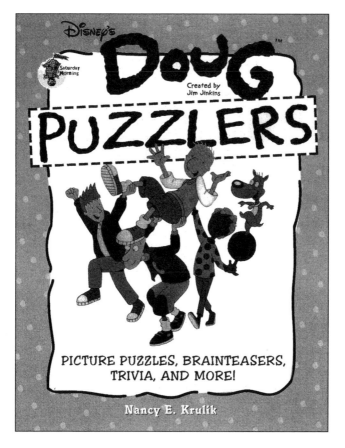

For more fun with puzzles, trivia, brainteasers, and more, look for Disney's Doug Puzzlers available in stores now.

$6.95 paperback